Violet Mackerel's

Possible Friend

Other stories about Violet Mackerel:

ANNA BRANFORD

illustrated by
SAM WILSON

WALKER
BOOKS

First published 2013 by Walker Books Australia Pty Ltd

First published in the UK 2014 by Walker Books Ltd
87 Vauxhall Walk, London SE11 5HJ

2 4 6 8 10 9 7 5 3 1

Text © 2013 Anna Branford
Illustrations © 2014 Sam Wilson

This book has been typeset in Bembo

Printed and bound in Great Britain by Clays Ltd, St Ives plc

British Library Cataloguing in Publication Data:
a catalogue record for this book is available from the British Library

ISBN 978-1-4063-4984-9

www.walker.co.uk

www.violetmackerel.com

For Holly (my niece)

AB

For Bella and Parker

SW

The Garden Fence

Violet Mackerel is exploring her new house. Her family has only just moved in, so she is discovering interesting things all the time.

Her first discovery in the new garden
is an ants' nest.
Hundreds of
ants crawl in and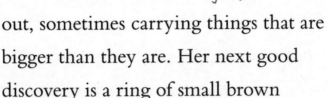
out, sometimes carrying things that are
bigger than they are. Her next good
discovery is a ring of small brown
mushrooms growing in a
damp spot. They look
like tiny umbrellas. But
the most interesting
discovery for the whole
morning is something that actually
looks very ordinary at first. It is a
brown knot in the pale wooden fence.
The knot is a dark circle with a ring
around it. Violet presses it like a button

to see if something happens,
but she doesn't really expect
that anything will. It moves.
She presses a little harder and it moves
a little more. She presses a little harder
still and suddenly it pops right through
the fence and falls out the other side.

Violet's heart does a jump. She looks
around to see if anyone has seen her
accidentally making a hole in the
fence. Luckily everyone is inside and
much too busy to notice anything.
No one has seen Violet
making the hole.
Perhaps, Violet thinks,
no one will guess it
was her.

One cheering thought is that she now has a good way of peeking into the garden next door. Mum says she thinks a girl lives there who is about Violet's age. Violet doesn't have any friends near the new house and she would quite like to make one.

But making a new friend can be tricky, especially if the possible person is someone you have never met or even seen before. Violet has been trying to think of some theories that might be helpful for friend-making, and her best idea so far is called the **Theory of Swapping Small Things**. The theory is that if two people give each other a small thing, they might end up becoming very good friends. She had the idea because when Mum and Vincent got married in their old garden, they gave each other small gold rings, which they both wear all the time. It was a good swap, Violet thinks, since now they are very special friends.

Violet doesn't have a spare ring, but she does have a few small things she could try swapping with the girl next door. Perhaps one of them would be perfect.

She squats down and puts her eye close to the hole, spying through it like a telescope.

The garden she sees is very different from her own, which is messy with lots of weeds and long grass because no one has had time to do any proper gardening yet. In the neighbours' garden there is no mess. There isn't a single weed or a slightly overgrown patch. It is the neatest, tidiest garden Violet has ever seen. It has a soft green lawn trimmed very short, with hedges clipped into special squarish shapes.

The owners must be very neat, tidy people, Violet thinks.

Then she has a slightly worrying thought. A family of tidy people might not be very pleased to discover a small hole in their fence.

Only a minute ago, Violet had been trying to think of a good small **thing** to swap with the girl next door. But now she is not thinking at all about making a new friend or testing her new theory. She is thinking about the tidy neighbours knocking crossly on the door and saying, "Why is there a hole in our fence and who put it there?" That is a *very* worrying thought.

When it gets near to bedtime, Violet is still worrying. She would quite like to tell Mum and Vincent about the hole before the neighbours come over. Mum and Vincent might be cross too, but they might also have some good ideas.

But everyone looks tired after a day of moving house. They are flopping on the couch and chairs, which aren't in quite the right spots yet, and watching the one flickery channel Nicola has managed to find on the new television. So Violet does not tell anybody about her worrying thought.

Something Violet particularly likes about the new house is that now she

has her own bunk bed. Violet slept
in a bunk bed once at a beach house
and has wanted one ever since. She
sleeps in the bottom bunk with a
sheet draped down so it makes a small
personal space. It is a good place
for thinking, even if the thinking is
mostly worrying, which it is tonight.
But before she goes to sleep Violet has
an idea about the problem of the hole
in the fence.

The Silver Bell

Sometimes when you wake up in the
morning and think about an idea you
had the night before,
it doesn't seem
quite as good.
At other times
it actually seems
better than it did

when you first thought of it. Violet's idea about the hole in the fence is the second sort.

Before she has had breakfast or even said hello to anyone, Violet looks through her **Box of** small **Things** and takes out a tiny silver bell. It is the kind that dangles on the bottom of an Indian skirt. If there are lots of them, they jingle when you walk. Violet only has one bell so it doesn't jingle, but she quite likes it and has been saving it for something important. She wraps it up in a small piece of purple tissue paper saved from a present Vincent once gave her. Then she sticks it together with a

sliver of sticky tape. It is the smallest
present she has ever wrapped.

Next Violet writes a message on a
piece of paper not much bigger than a
postage stamp, using her tiniest, tiniest
handwriting. She writes:

Then she draws a tiny violet and
folds up the note. It is the smallest note
she has ever written.

Violet takes the present and the note

out into the garden and puts them in the hole in the fence. They rest perfectly in the curve of the wood.

Her idea is that if a person notices something like a hole in their fence, they would probably go over and look at it closely. And if they find an apologizing note and a small present waiting there, perhaps they are less likely to mind too much. It is a good idea, Violet thinks.

When everybody else gets up, there are lots of things to do. Dylan has a violin exam in the afternoon, so he is practising nearly every minute and it is Violet's job to turn the pages of the music book for him. Dylan cannot talk at the same time as playing the violin, not even just to say "turn the page now, please". He wrinkles his nose when it is nearly time for Violet to turn the page. Violet listens to the music, watches Dylan's nose very carefully and thinks and thinks about the present in the hole in the fence.

Mum has been knitting owls for a friend's shop and they have to be finished by the afternoon, but they don't have eyes yet because she has been so busy unpacking. So Violet helps with the eyes and then in the afternoon she and Mum deliver the owls together.

It is a shop Violet likes and usually she is glad when Mum stops for a chat with her friend because that means there is time to look around.

But this afternoon Violet is thinking non-stop about the tidy neighbours and wondering if they have noticed the hole or found the note and the silver bell. So even though there are a lot of new and interesting things in the shop, like crocheted cupcakes and doughnuts, and notebooks with felt ladybirds on the covers, which Violet especially likes, most of all she just wants to go home.

So, as soon as they get back, Violet runs out to the garden. She can see from quite a few steps away that there is still a tiny tissue-wrapped present and note in the hole. She is slightly relieved because it means that the tidy neighbours probably haven't noticed. But she is also a bit disappointed because it would have been nice for them to find the silver bell and not be cross.

However, when she gets closer to the fence and looks more carefully, Violet notices something very interesting. The tissue parcel in the hole is not purple any more. It is *pink*.

The Pink Parcel

Violet takes the pink tissue parcel out of the hole. There is also a tiny note. Mum says it is polite to open cards before presents, but as far as Violet knows there are no rules about notes and, anyway, no one is there to be polite for. So she unwraps the pink parcel first, peeling away a sliver of sticky tape. Even though she is very curious, she opens it slowly and carefully, trying not to tear the tissue.

Inside the parcel is a beautiful purple gemstone. It is about the size of Violet's little fingernail. She knows the proper name for it because Nicola has some precious gemstone beads and a book that tells you which stones are which. Nicola has shown the book to Violet, so Violet knows that the icy purple ones are called *amethysts*.

They are her favourite of all the gemstones. It is a very good present, she thinks.

Next she unfolds the tiny note.
The handwriting is a little bit like hers,
but neater. It says:

Hello Violet,
Thank you for the lovely bell.
Don't worry about the hole.
I am not cross and no one
has noticed except me.
Here is a present for you too.
Would you like to come over
tomorrow morning?
From Rose

At the bottom of the note is a tiny
drawing of a rose.

Violet folds the note up, wraps the
amethyst back in the pink tissue and

puts them both in her pocket. But she keeps taking them out and looking at them again and again.

Although Violet does not want to tell anyone the secret of the hole in the fence, she does tell Mum about Rose's invitation. (If you don't mention where an invitation comes from, even a strangely small one, people usually don't ask you any questions about it.) Mum says she can go, so Violet puts another note in the hole that says *Yes, please*, signed with a violet. Later on, Mum knocks on the new neighbours' door to see what time Violet should come and also to borrow a can opener, since the Mackerels' can opener is still in a box somewhere and no one can find it.

Violet does not go with Mum because she wants to do some planning before she meets Rose for the first time. Since they have swapped small things, perhaps they will become very good friends. And on the day you meet a very good friend for the first time, Violet thinks it might be important to wear something special.

In her new room there is a box of old clothes that Nicola has outgrown. Mum says most of them will still be a bit big for Violet, but Violet

has been having seconds of dinner
quite a lot lately, and she might be
bigger than people think. In the box
she finds a skirt that used to be Nicola's
favourite. It is dark purple and when
Nicola twirled in it very
fast, it flew out into
a perfect fluttering
circle. Violet tries
the skirt on. She
breathes out as much
as she can
but the
skirt is
still quite
loose. Then
she has the idea

of pegging it at the side with a wooden clothes peg. She twirls and it flies out perfectly.

Violet has a red-and-white stripy top that is long enough to cover the peg. She tries it on and looks in the mirror on the inside of her wardrobe door. All you can see of the peg is a slight lump at the side. It is a good outfit for meeting a possible very good friend for the first time, Violet thinks.

She lays it all out on her chair ready for tomorrow and puts the small amethyst in the pocket of the stripy top. Then she puts her pyjamas on and wishes and wishes that the morning would hurry up.

Before she goes to bed she checks the hole in the fence one more time. There is a new note. It says, *See you tomorrow!*, signed with a rose. Violet hopes and hopes that Rose might turn out to be a very good friend.

The Missing Sock

Violet wakes up so early
the next morning that it is
still a bit dark outside.
She gets dressed
straight away in
her skirt and top. She
wishes she could find
both of her favourite

purple socks instead of only one
purple sock and one stripy sock.
But when she puts her boots on you
can hardly tell that her socks don't
match. She chooses some books from
the pile Mum unpacked yesterday and
waits for the sun to rise properly.

When the sun is finally all the way
up and there are shuffling noises
and the sound of the kettle on in the
kitchen, Violet runs downstairs. After
breakfast, she puts some muffins that
she and Vincent made very carefully
into a box to take to Rose's house.

At last, it is time to go next door.
Mum comes too, to return the
borrowed can opener. Violet is glad

because even when you have really been looking forward to meeting someone for the first time, you can get slight butterflies when it actually happens. It is nice if someone goes with you, at least as far as the door.

Violet rings the doorbell and Rose's mum answers. A lovely smell of perfume wafts out onto the porch. Rose's mum has red lipstick on and is wearing a perfectly white blouse

without any wrinkles, like someone on television. Violet suspects Mum's shirt was once white too, but now it is quite a lot of different colours. It is the one she wears to do things like painting and unpacking boxes, so there are also quite a few wrinkles.

While Mum gives back the can opener and they chat for quite a long time, Violet stands behind Mum and peeps. Sometimes she peeps at exactly the same moment as the girl who is standing behind Rose's mum, peeping too. She is wearing a crisp pale pink dress like a girl in a magazine.

When it happens a few times in a row they both get the giggles. After that, when Rose's mum says, "Rose, why don't you take Violet upstairs and show her your room?", Rose says, "Come in, Violet!" and Violet runs inside as though they are already very good friends.

Even though Rose is jiggling a little bit and doing an excited sort of squeak, her dress stays as unwrinkly as her mum's blouse. She even has matching pale pink hairclips. Violet puts her hand over her peg lump.

"We take our shoes off indoors," says Rose, quickly. "It's so the carpet doesn't get ruined."

Violet takes her boots off and puts them beside a neat row of shoes near the door. She wishes very much that she had been able to find her other favourite sock, or in fact any two socks that were the same. Rose's socks match perfectly and they are white with a pink rose on each ankle. Violet does a little swallow and follows Rose up the soft, carpeted stairs to her room.

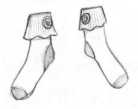

The Doll's House

Violet has never been
in a room like Rose's
before. Everything
is pink or white
or both, and her
bed has a floaty
curtain all around
called a canopy.

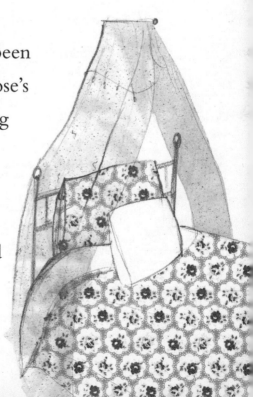

There is an oval mirror on a stand
that can tilt backwards and forwards,
and a dresser with pink crystal knobs.
And beside the dresser on a pink rug is
the loveliest doll's house Violet has ever
seen. Even though Rose wants to show
her lots of other beautiful things, Violet
cannot stop looking at the doll's house.

"Want to see inside?" Rose asks.

"Yes, please!" says Violet.

Rose pulls
out the doll's
house and a
box of dolls
and furniture.
Violet tucks
her differently

socked feet underneath her and looks, not daring to touch.

There is a tiny grand piano, a lampshade, an oven with pots and pans, a bath with gold taps, a sofa, a dining table with chairs and even a cheese platter with cheeses and a silver knife.

"Do you have a doll's house?" asks Rose.

Violet does have one that she and Nicola made in a shoebox. They made a chest of drawers by sticking matchboxes together and gluing on beads for knobs, and they made a mirror by covering a tiddlywink in silver foil. But even though she does have a sort of doll's house, Violet says,

"No," quite softly, since she suspects that the shoebox sort doesn't count.

"How about you set up the living room," says Rose. "And I'll set up the bedroom."

Violet likes choosing the pieces of furniture from the box and deciding where they should go. Rose sets up a tiny canopy bed, a pink rug and a little tilting mirror on a stand.

"That looks just like your bedroom!" says Violet.

"I know," says Rose. "I've been collecting the pieces for ages. I wish there was a dresser like mine though." Rose puts a plain white one in the doll's house bedroom. "They don't make them with pink crystal knobs."

Violet decorates the living room
with a grandfather clock and some
bookshelves with books on them.
Rose does her excited squeak when
she sees how it all looks. It is so much
fun working on the doll's house with
Rose and so interesting to try and
read the tiny writing on the books
that Violet forgets to worry
about her socks. When
she kneels right down
to look through the
doorway into the
kitchen she forgets
to worry about
her peg too.

"Why do you have a peg on your skirt?" asks Rose.

Violet pulls her stripy top back down as far as it will go.

"It's my sister's old skirt and it's still a bit big for me," she says, wishing and wishing that she had a perfect dress like Rose's.

"That's a clever idea," says Rose. She looks thoughtfully at the peg lump.

Violet and Rose have their morning snack sitting on special high stools beside the kitchen counter. There is a fresh pine foresty smell and a nice soft hum coming from the dishwasher. The only thing on the shiny kitchen counter is a brochure from a bakery, open to some pink-and-white cupcakes with sugar flowers on top. Violet thinks about the box of muffins she and Vincent made and wonders if Rose normally has iced cupcakes with flowers for morning tea.

"Mum is ordering those for my birthday party," says Rose.

"They're beautiful," says Violet. She would like to taste one but she suspects Rose probably doesn't invite peg-wearers to her parties.

Rose's mum pours their
juice into tall glasses and adds
ice cubes from a special box in
the freezer using tongs. Violet watches
carefully. She has never had ice from
tongs before and somehow it looks
nicer than ordinary ice. The muffins
Violet brought look very plain next
to the cupcakes in the picture, even
though Violet chose the best ones to
bring. But Rose and her mum both eat
two and say they are delicious.

After their snack they go back to the
doll's house and Violet has the idea of
taking the small amethyst out of her
pocket and putting it on the table as a
centrepiece. That gives Rose the idea

of taking the tiny silver bell out of her treasure pouch and hanging it on the door as a doorbell.

Rose squeaks and Violet does a small squeak too, just to see what it feels like.

Later on, when Mum knocks on the real door and says it is time for Violet to come home, instead of packing up the doll's house, Rose says they should slide it carefully back beside the dresser as it is, so they can keep working on it another day. The only things they change are the amethyst, which goes back into Violet's pocket and the silver bell, which goes back into Rose's treasure pouch.

Violet smiles, even though it is time to leave and she would much rather stay. The **Theory of Swapping Small Things** might be quite a good theory, she thinks. But she is still not sure.

The
Pot Plant Gecko

In the afternoon,
after doing some
more unpacking and
organizing, Violet
and Mum sit down for
a cool drink and Violet would like to
put ice in hers. She looks in the new
freezer in case there is a special icebox
like Rose's, but there is just a normal

plastic tray of ice. Violet asks Mum if there are any little silver ice tongs in the boxes they haven't unpacked yet. Mum says not as far as she knows.

While they have their tray-ice drinks in ordinary glasses, Violet tells Mum about Rose's lovely tall glasses, the special no-shoes carpet, the shiny kitchen counter and the perfect flowery cupcakes Rose is having at her party. Mum says, "How lovely," but she says it in a slightly tired way. Violet tells her about Rose's crystal-knob dresser with no dust on it, the pine forest smell and the nice hum of the dishwasher. Mum seems to look even more exhausted than when she first sat down.

Just as Violet is asking if Mum would like to hear about the fluffy towels and the special liquid soap she saw in Rose's bathroom, Vincent comes in and says, "I bet Rose doesn't have a gecko in her pot plant," and they all go out onto the back porch to see the tiny lizard he has found. It has a nice, friendly face and small suckers on its feet that Violet quite likes. She wonders if Rose would be interested in seeing a lizard so tiny that it could easily fit in your pocket.

As she thinks about it, she puts her
hand in her pocket and her fingers
twiddle the small piece of amethyst
Rose gave her. If Rose liked the gecko,
she might also like to see some of the
other interesting things Violet has
found at the new house, like the ants'
nest and the ring of little umbrella
mushrooms. She might even like to see
Violet's new room and her bunk bed.
So Violet asks Mum and Vincent if she
can invite Rose over, and they say yes.

Violet writes a small note asking if
Rose would like to come over. Rose
will be her first guest at the new house
and that is quite special, so she draws
some stars around the message before

putting the note in
the hole in the fence.
But as she goes back
through the garden
to her house, Violet
thinks again of how
messy it is compared with Rose's
beautiful, neat garden.

Violet's room is not pink and white
and her things do not match like
Rose's. They are all different and
maybe Rose won't think that is as nice.
There will only be normal ice and
ordinary soap for Rose to use. And
another worrying thought is the doll's
house. Violet wonders what Rose will
think about being very good friends

with someone who turns out to have a doll's house that is the shoebox sort.

Violet twiddles the amethyst and thinks of the gecko, and there are some hopeful thoughts in among her worrying ones.

Very soon the note disappears and Violet finds another one saying,

Dear Violet,
Yes please! I will
see you tomorrow.
From Rose

The
Party Invitation

The next day when there is
finally a knock at the door,
Violet runs down
to answer it. Violet
says that Rose
doesn't have to
take off her shoes
because the carpet is
not the special sort

and Rose looks quite pleased. Even though Violet feels a bit shy about showing Rose around a house which smells more like toast than a fresh pine forest, it is actually quite fun giving her a tour because Rose is so curious about everything and does her excited squeak lots of times.

Rose is interested in all the things Violet points out, like the ring of mushrooms, the ants' nest in the garden and the Indian curtains Mum is hanging up that Vincent brought back from Mumbai. But she is also very interested in things that Violet herself hardly notices, like the yoghurt Vincent is making in a bowl in the kitchen.

It's what Violet has for breakfast every morning, so she had not thought of showing it to Rose. But Rose has never seen anyone make yoghurt before and asks Vincent lots of questions about it.

Rose is very interested in Mum's knitting basket too. It is full of some toadstools she is making to go in the shop Violet likes. A few of them still need spots and some don't even have their stuffing in yet.

"I can't believe your mum actually *makes* these," says

Rose, picking up a toadstool as carefully as if it was a baby bird.

"She can knit owls and gnomes and fish too," says Violet. "And also rabbits."

Best of all, Rose likes Violet's room. Violet shows her the blue china bird Vincent gave her and the flower girl dress with wings that Mum made for her out of a nightie.

They take Violet's **Box of** Small **Things** into the personal

Violet's box of small things

space in Violet's bunk bed, which Rose says is like being in a real tent. Violet has never shared that space with anyone before, but it is nice to sit there with Rose, especially when she spots a button shaped like a tiny rose and does one of her excited squeaks.

Later on, after Violet has shown Rose how to make her own **Box of Small Things**, Rose's mum knocks at the door and Vincent invites her in for a cup of tea. Rose's mum says it has been a long day and that would be very nice, so Mum makes a pot and Vincent puts out the rest of the leftover muffins.

Rose watches Mum spooning tea leaves into the teapot.

"Do we have tea leaves at our house, Mum, or just ordinary tea bags?" asks Rose.

"Just ordinary tea bags, I think," says Rose's mum.

"Did you know Violet and Vincent *made* these muffins?" Rose asks. "And they make yoghurt too and Violet has it every day for breakfast!"

"How lovely," says Rose's mum, in a slightly tired way.

"And Violet's mum makes all kinds of things too," says Rose. "She can knit toadstools with spots, and owls and gnomes and fish. And she made Violet a flower girl dress with wings!"

Rose's mum seems to look even more exhausted than when she first sat down.

Vincent suggests that Violet gets the gecko from the pot plant, since it is becoming quite tame now and Rose hasn't seen it yet. Everyone looks at its friendly face and the little suckers on its feet. Rose would like to have a turn holding it and she squeaks when Vincent puts it very gently in her hands. The two mums have more tea and talk for quite a long time.

That evening, a little while after Rose has gone home, Violet finds a note waiting for her in the hole in the fence. It looks more special than the other notes because it is on pink paper with sparkly edges, and instead of being folded, it is curled into a scroll.

It says:

Dear Violet,
You are invited to my birthday
party on Saturday at 11.00.
It is a flower party so you can
dress up as any flower you like.
I am going to be a rose, so
maybe you could be a violet.
I hope you can come!
From Rose

Violet twiddles the piece of amethyst
in her pocket.

The Matchbox Dresser

Violet is quite excited about the invitation. She has never been to a flower party before and she thinks about possible violet costumes she could make. She has a few good ideas. But then she has a very different kind of thought. What if

Rose and her guests all have the sorts
of costumes you get from an actual
fancy dress shop? What if they all look
like real flowers and Violet is the only
one at the party wearing green tights
and a purple hand-me-down skirt?
Suddenly Violet's mind fills up
with worries again.

After she has
worried for a little
while about her
costume, Violet starts
thinking about what sort of birthday
present she will give to Rose. Usually,
Mum or Nicola help her to make
birthday presents for people's parties,
like a peg doll or a beaded bookmark

or a library bag with the person's name
sewn on it. Even though Violet thinks
those are all very good presents, she
can't quite imagine any of them being
in Rose's beautiful room. Perhaps
other guests at the party will bring big
presents and they will all be pink and
white. And Violet might only have
a small present to bring, which might
not be pink *or* white. That is a *very*
worrying thought.

"You're very quiet this evening,
Violet," says Vincent at dinnertime.
Everyone has been talking about plans
for the new garden and Violet has not
been talking about anything at all.
"Is there something the matter?"

"No," says Violet. Her voice sounds a bit cross, even though she doesn't really feel it. When your mind is full of worrying thoughts, it can be difficult to talk about ordinary things like whether or not there should be a barbecue and a special outdoor table and chairs, and sometimes that makes your voice sound cross.

Later on, at bedtime, while Mum is tucking Violet in, she says, "Are you sure nothing is wrong, Violet? You don't seem like yourself tonight."

"I seem exactly like myself tonight," says Violet. She sounds cross again, even though she still isn't really. "Just a self with some worrying thoughts."

"Sometimes worries don't seem as bad if you tell someone about them," says Mum.

"Unless they say, 'That is a silly thing to worry about,'" points out Violet.

"What if I promise not to say that?" suggests Mum.

So Violet tells Mum about the problems of the costume and the present.

Mum thinks for a little while. "A good way of making yourself feel worried is by thinking about what you don't have and can't do," she says, "but a good trick for feeling better again is by thinking about what you *do* have and *can* do."

Violet wishes very, very much that she had a perfect violet costume and a present for Rose that was as big and beautiful as the doll's house. But as she goes to sleep, she tries Mum's trick.

And in the morning Violet has an idea. She looks around the house for matchboxes. Vincent has some in his old camping kit and he doesn't mind tipping the nearly empty ones into the nearly full ones. He gives Violet three boxes. Nicola keeps her jewellery-making supplies in matchboxes, so she has quite a collection and gives Violet another two. And Violet herself has one in her **Box of** Small **Things**. Six is enough, she thinks.

She glues the matchboxes in two stacks of three and sticks a piece of stiff white card across the top like the surface of a dresser. Then she cuts a strip off some beautiful white pearly paper from a wedding invitation that someone sent to Mum. Violet has been saving it for something special. She wraps it around the sides of the boxes and glues it in place. It is a very good mini dresser but it does look a bit like the plain white one

that Rose already has. That is because Violet has not finished yet.

In Nicola's book about gemstones, Violet's second favourite stone after the amethyst is the icy pink gem called the rose quartz. Nicola has some rose quartz pieces in one of her matchboxes and Violet hopes Nicola might give her six very small rose quartz beads.

It is quite a good time to ask Nicola for things because her room in the new house is bigger than her old one and she is very happy about it. People quite often say yes to things when they are already feeling happy. So even though the rose quartz beads are quite precious, Nicola doesn't mind giving six to

Violet. She also lends Violet her special glue that dries very quickly. With the pink crystal knobs on the drawers, the dresser looks almost like Rose's real one. Not exactly, but almost.

When the dresser is finished, Violet shows it to Vincent. He looks closely and opens the drawers very carefully by their rose quartz knobs.

"Do you think it's a good enough present for Rose?" Violet asks him.

"I think it's a good enough present for anybody," says Vincent.

"Not all people like homemade presents," says Violet, worrying again.

"But some people like that sort of present the best," says Vincent. "I do."

Violet hopes that Rose is that kind of person too.

Next, Violet asks Nicola about the flower costume, hoping that she is happy enough about her new room to help with two worries. Nicola thinks the purple skirt is just right and she has a green top she can lend Violet that is only slightly too big and will hide the peg completely. She also has a pair of stripy purple socks. When Violet tries it all on, she does look quite a lot like an upside-down violet.

Nicola has another idea too. Violet once helped her to cut out felt leaves as part of a school project and Nicola thinks they could make some similar leaves for Violet's costume. They cut heart-shaped leaves out of green felt and stick them onto hairpins. When the glue has dried and Nicola puts the pins in Violet's hair, she actually looks almost *exactly* like an upside-down violet. Finally, Nicola puts one of her own clear quartz necklaces around Violet's neck. The small, watery beads look like morning dewdrops on violet petals. "Do you think this will be all right to wear to Rose's party?" Violet asks Nicola.

"The others will probably have fancy-dress-shop costumes."

"I think it will be fine," says Nicola. "And I bet you will be the only flower with dewdrops."

Violet hopes Nicola is right.

There is just enough felt left to cut out three small, jagged rose leaf shapes to put on hairpins so Rose can have leaves in her hair too, if she likes. They fit nicely in the drawers of the matchbox chest.

For Rose's birthday card, Violet draws a violet and a rose. She looks at the card and twiddles the amethyst in

her pocket. Then she draws a ribbon
tied in a bow around the two flowers.
She hopes Rose will like it.

Mostly, though, Violet is hoping
that she will not be the only person at
the party whose costume is not from
a proper fancy dress shop. Also she
hopes that at least one other person at
the party will only have a small present
for Rose.

The Birthday Party

On the morning of the party, Violet's hopes seem to fade away like a small splash of water on a very hot day.

She puts the matchbox dresser right at the back of her cupboard with the shoebox doll's house.

She puts the violet costume away with her very ordinary clothes.

And at breakfast, when Mum suggests a big bowl of muesli and yoghurt to give her extra energy for the party, Violet says quietly, "I'm not going to the party."

"Then what will you do with that clever matchbox dresser you made?" asks Vincent.

"Nothing," says Violet. And it is a very sad thought, because she worked very hard to make it.

"You might not get the chance to wear your violet costume again for a long time," said Nicola. "Not many people have flower parties."

"I don't mind," said Violet.

But actually, it is another sad thought. Violet has never heard of anyone besides Rose having a flower party.

"Did you make Rose a card?" asks Dylan. He is very good at drawing and he likes looking at other people's drawings.

Violet is too sad to eat even a very small bowl of muesli and yoghurt, so she goes upstairs to get the card she made to show Dylan.

"A violet and a rose," says Dylan. "You actually made

the ribbon curl around like a real ribbon does. Look, Mum!"

Mum comes around to look at the curling ribbon. "What a beautiful card," she says. "I think Rose would love it."

"Really?" asks Violet.

"Really," says Mum.

"Well, maybe I'll go for a little while, just to see what it's like," says Violet. She puts on her costume and wraps up the matchbox dresser with the leaf hairclips tucked inside. Mum gives her some pink rosy ribbon to tie the parcel with. And then it is time to go.

Violet takes a deep breath.
Standing on the doorstep,
she can hear lots of voices
inside Rose's house. Rose's
mum answers the door,
dressed up as a hibiscus
flower with a red dress
and a sort of yellow
crown for the stalky
part in the middle. It is a
very, very beautiful costume
and definitely the kind that
comes from a fancy dress shop.
Violet does a little swallow.

Violet follows her inside
and straight away sees
another grown-up with

a very beautiful costume.
It is a daisy dress with a
bright yellow bodice, a stiff
white petal tutu and white
petal wings on the back.
There are little green
silk slippers which must be all
right on the special carpet, Violet
thinks, because the daisy is wearing
them inside. Her face is painted
with tiny sparking daisies. Violet does
a big swallow and looks down at her
purple woolly socks. She could still
run back home.

"Hello, Violet!" squeaks
Rose. "This is the flower fairy
face painter for my party!"

The daisy, whose actual name is Simone, has a little suitcase full of paints and brushes and glitter. She is trying to paint a sparkly rose on Rose's cheek with a tiny paintbrush and she is laughing and asking Rose to keep her face still, but Rose can't because she keeps wanting to smile at Violet. That makes Violet feel a bit better, but only a bit.

A daffodil, a tulip, a fuchsia and a lily are crowding around waiting for their turn and while they all wait and watch, a dandelion and a forget-me-not arrive and crowd around too.

The daffodil has a headdress with big yellow petals blooming out all

round her face
and the fuschia
looks like a
ballerina with
a pink-and-purple
petal dress and red
tights so her legs look
like dangling stamens.
Rose herself has a swirly pink silk skirt
that looks as soft as real rose petals.

But there are some other costumes
too. A slightly gloomy-looking boy
in a green tracksuit is supposed to be
a cornflower but he doesn't want to
wear his blue hat so he is just being
a stalk. One girl has an antennae
headband and a skirt with black spots.

She says she didn't have a flower
costume so she has come as a ladybird,
and someone giggles.

"Ladybirds live in flowers," says
Violet, who knows quite a bit about
ladybirds. "I think it's a good costume
for a flower party."

The ladybird smiles
and lets Violet try
on her antennae while
Simone paints a sparkly
bug on her face.

Soon it is Violet's turn to have her
face painted. While she is keeping
still so her violet doesn't get smudged,
she watches other people giving Rose
their presents. The daffodil gives her

a matching jewellery set with a locket. Rose squeaks happily. The forget-me-not gives her a nail polish kit and a little fan for drying your nails. Rose squeaks even more. Violet looks sadly at her small present. Rose will not squeak when she opens it. Violet does not want to give it to her at all. So when no one is looking, she hides it behind a vase.

Her only hope now is that there are so many big presents from her very good friends that Rose might not notice if there is none from just a possible friend. No present is probably better than a dresser made of matchboxes, Violet thinks.

Next, Simone shows everyone a game where she puts lots of flowers on a tray and then covers them all up and you have to remember as many of the different kinds as you can. They play other games too and people win glittery pens and flower bangles. Even though Violet isn't really concentrating she wins a notebook for pinning the poppy on the stem with a blindfold on. The stalk looks gloomy again after winning hairclips in a layer of pass-the-parcel, so Violet gives him her notebook. She doesn't mind because she suspects you shouldn't really win a prize if you don't give a present. The stalk looks a bit less gloomy after that.

Then they have the birthday cupcakes, which look even more beautiful than they did in the brochure, with sparklers and candles burning between them for Rose to blow out while everyone sings "Happy Birthday".

After the cakes everyone goes outside into Rose's beautiful garden to play a game where you have to stand back and throw the wishing pebble into the sunflower. If it lands in the petals you get to keep the pebble and if it lands the middle, Simone gives you a much more special pebble with a flower painted on it.

It is a good game, Violet thinks, and she would like to win a pebble. But much more than that, she would like to go home.

Violet goes over to Rose and taps her on the shoulder, to tell the small fib of a slight headache and to say an early goodbye. But before she can say anything, Rose squeaks and whispers something in her ear.

The Thank You Note

"Come inside for a minute. I want to show you something," whispers Rose. Everyone is busy, so no one notices them disappearing into the house and up the stairs together.

Violet wonders if Rose has a whole street of pink-and-white doll's houses to show her. On the way, Violet grabs her present from behind the vase. If you only have a small thing to give someone, it can be easier without everyone watching.

There are a few new birthday things in Rose's room. There are white cushions on her canopy bed that spell out R–O–S–E in pink letters and there is a shiny new car beside the doll's house. But those are not what Rose wants to show Violet.

"Look!" says Rose, pulling up her green top, which has pointy bits all around the neck, to show Violet the

top of her beautiful swirly
rose-pink skirt. At the side
there is a wooden peg.

"It's my mum's skirt," says Rose.
"She said we could get it made the
right size for the party, but I wanted
a peg so it would be like yours."

Violet puts down the present and
pulls up her green top to show her
matching peg. It is a funny surprise but
a very nice one. They both twirl and
their skirts fly out in fluttering circles.

"I wish I had leaves in my hair," says
Rose, admiring Violet's. "Then we
would *really* match."

Violet takes a deep breath and picks
up her present. She does an enormous

swallow. Then she holds it out
to Rose.

"It's only very small," she says.

Rose opens the card Violet made.
"A rose and a violet! That's us!" she
says. Then she carefully unwraps
the present. Suddenly her eyes get
very big.

"It's my dresser!" she squeaks.
She holds it up to compare it with
her own actual dresser. "It's perfect!"
She squeaks again and does some
slight twirling.

Violet is so happy she wants to
squeak and twirl too.

Rose pulls out the doll's house to put
the dresser in the bedroom right away,

but Violet says, "Look inside the drawers first."

Pulling open the drawers with the tiny rose quartz knobs, Rose takes out the little jagged leaf hairclips and squeaks even more. Violet puts them in her hair and they look at themselves in Rose's special tilting mirror. They are a matching leafy rose and violet, like the ones on the card Violet made.

Rose gives Violet a thank-you hug and they put the matchbox dresser in the doll's house. It is a very good fit. Then they run back downstairs. No one has even noticed they were missing.

After that it feels like almost no time before the parents start arriving to pick everyone up and the party is over. Violet says goodbye to the ladybird and the stalk and thank you to Simone and Rose's mum. Rose just says goodbye and thank you to most of the guests as they leave, but she gives Violet another big hug.

No one needs to pick Violet up because she is only walking back next door.

"Did you have a good time?" asks Mum later on, while Violet is in the bath, carefully washing around the sparkly violet on her cheek.

"I had a very good time," says Violet.

That evening in the hole in the fence, she finds a note from Rose saying thank you again for the dresser and the hairclips. It is addressed to "My very good friend Violet" and at the bottom is a picture of a violet and a rose, tied together with a ribbon. Violet twiddles the piece of amethyst in her pocket. The **Theory of Swapping** Small **Things** might be quite a good theory, she thinks.

More
Violet Mackerel
stories to collect:

Violet thinks she would QUITE LIKE to own the blue china bird at the Saturday market.

But what she needs is a PLOT.

A BRILLIANT plot...

Violet has to have her tonsils out.

And that's all right, because maybe Violet will make the most REMARKABLE RECOVERY ever.

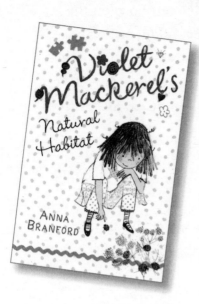

Violet Mackerel quite likes helping.

But sometimes it's hard to know the best way to help a SMALL THING - especially when it's not in its NATURAL HABITAT.

Violet Mackerel has some GOOD news and some NOT-SO-GOOD news.

Violet is trying to be brave, but sometimes leaving your PERSONAL SPACE can be tricky.

ANNA BRANFORD was born on the Isle of Man, but spent her childhood in Sudan, Papua New Guinea and Australia. Once, when she was very itchy with the chicken pox, her dad read her *The Very Hungry Caterpillar* thirty times in a row.

Anna lectures in Sociology at Victoria University, Australia, and spends her evenings writing children's stories, kept company by a furry black cat called Florence. She also makes dolls using recycled fabric and materials.

SAM WILSON graduated from Kingston University in 1999 and has since been working on lots of grown-up books. The Violet Mackerel books are the first titles she has illustrated for children. She says, "I have always wanted to illustrate for children, it has been such fun drawing Violet, she is a gorgeous character with such an adventurous spirit." Sam lives in the countryside with her husband, two children, a black Lab called Jess and several chickens.